# DANGEROUS GAMES

# MIDNIGHT MANSION

Sue Graves

RISING ★ STARS

Rising Stars UK Ltd.
7 Hatchers Mews, Bermonds
www.risingstars-uk.com

nasen

NASEN House, 4/5 Amber Business Village, Amber Close,
Amington, Tamworth, Staffordshire B77 4RP

Text, design and layout © Rising Stars UK Ltd.

Published 2012

Author: Sue Graves
Series editor: Sasha Morton
Text and logo design: pentacorbig
Typesetting: Geoff Rayner, Bag of Badgers
Cover design: Lon Chan
Publisher: Gill Budgell
Project Manager: Sasha Morton Creative Project Management
Editorial: Deborah Kespert
Artwork: Colour: Lon Chan / B&W: Paul Loudon

British Library Cataloguing in Publication Data.
A CIP record for this book is available from the British Library.

ISBN: 978-0-85769-611-3

Printed by Craftprint International, Singapore

# CHAPTER 1

It was Friday night and Tom and Sima were at Kojo's flat. They were all really tired. It had been a very busy week at the office and now they just wanted to chill out and relax. They worked at Dangerous Games, a computer games company, and they were all good mates.

Tom, Sima and Kojo worked as a team. Sima was the designer, Kojo programmed the games and Tom tested them. They thought they had the best jobs ever, but Tom was always boasting that he had the best job of all.

"Right guys," said Tom. "Let me show you what I have for your entertainment this evening." He pulled out a DVD from his bag and loaded it onto Kojo's DVD player.

Sima yawned. "I think I just want to curl up on the sofa and go to sleep," she said.

"Yeah, me too," said Kojo. He stretched out and rubbed his eyes.

Tom grinned. "You won't feel like sleeping when you've watched this!" he said.

"What's it about?" asked Sima, plumping up a cushion and putting it behind her head.

"It's all about a place called Chillington Mansion and it's said to be one of the most haunted houses on the planet," said Tom. "It'll be brilliant."

"Rubbish!" snorted Kojo. "There are no such things as ghosts."

"Well, this film is about real-life hauntings at Chillington Mansion," said Tom. "So let's just watch it and then we can judge for ourselves whether we think it's true or not."

Sima, Tom and Kojo settled down to watch the film, but it was really scary. Ghosts moaned and groaned and wailed and shrieked. Some walked through walls and some dragged chains behind them. Some even carried their heads under their arms.

The worst part was when the screen went black and there was an ear-splitting scream. Sima even hid behind her cushion! But when she looked up a few seconds later, she couldn't see the boys anywhere.

Suddenly, she heard a sound. Sima peered over the top of her cushion and saw Tom and Kojo cowering behind the sofa. They looked really scared.

"You big babies," she laughed. "Don't tell me you're frightened of a silly old film."

Just then another scream, louder than before, shrieked from the television. Sima jumped over the sofa in one giant leap.

"So you're not scared either!" laughed Tom, giving her a shove. "That's why you're shaking like a leaf."

"You're not funny," said Sima, pushing him away. "Turn off the film. I don't want to watch it any more." Then she grinned. "But it has given me a good idea for a new game."

# CHAPTER 2

On Monday morning, Sima was in the office early. By the time Tom and Kojo arrived, she had already loaded up Kojo's computer with the plans she had been working on over the weekend.

"Right, sit down you two," she ordered, when the boys had taken off their coats. "I'm going to run through the new game. It's called Midnight Mansion."

"This should be good," remarked Tom and he winked at Kojo.

"The game has three players," said Sima, "and they have to work as a team."

"Nice!" said Kojo. "We don't often have team games."

"The game is set in a booby-trapped haunted house at midnight," continued Sima, "and it will be played entirely in the dark."

"I can already see a problem," said Kojo, shaking his head. "Playing in the dark isn't practical. How will three players be able to work as a team if they can't see each other?"

"I've thought of that," said Sima. "To make the game possible, each player will be given night-vision glasses."

"Oh yeah!" said Tom. "I love it when we have extra gadgets in the games."

"But that's not all," continued Sima. "The players will also be given headsets so they can keep in contact with each other. They will only hear the 'Game Over' message that takes them out of the game through the headsets. Simple!"

"That is sooo cool!" said Tom and he punched the air. "This game is going to be awesome."

"But what's the aim of the game?" asked Kojo.

"Good question," said Sima. "The aim is to try and escape from the haunted house before the game time runs out. The only exit is through the main door."

"What happens if you don't?" asked Kojo.

"What happens if you don't what?" said Sima.

"You know," said Kojo, "get out of the game on time."

Sima shivered and looked worried. She took a deep breath. "If players don't get out on time, they will be trapped in the house forever."

"You're kidding!" gasped Kojo.

"No, I'm afraid not," replied Sima. "There's no other way I can design the game. That is how it has to be."

Later that morning, Kojo set to work on programming the game. Everything went well and he was really pleased.

"At this rate, it should be ready for testing tomorrow," he said. "I take it we are planning to test the game for real?"

"You bet," said Tom. "This is one game I can't wait to test. Have you got the night-vision glasses and headsets sorted?"

"Nearly," said Kojo. "I've just got a few tiny tweaks to make on the headsets and then we'll be good to go."

"I've got a great idea," said Tom.

"Uh oh!" said Sima. "I don't like the sound of that."

"If we're going to test the game for real, why don't we test it in real time, too?"

"What, at midnight?" said Sima.

"Yes, it'll be amazing," said Tom.

"But what about my beauty sleep?" said Sima. "I need eight hours of sleep at night or I get really grumpy."

"It'll be so exciting to play in the dark. Come on, Sima. I think I could put up with you being grumpy just this once," said Tom.

Sima grinned and rolled her eyes. "OK," she sighed. "Midnight it is."

The next evening Sima, Tom and Kojo stayed behind after work. Tom ordered a pizza and Sima made lots of hot coffee. Mr Wilson, their boss, came into the office to see what was going on.

"Not going home tonight?" he asked. "What are you up to?"

"We want to do some overtime on our new game, Mr Wilson," said Kojo. "We're really keen to get it right."

"That's what I like to see," smiled Mr Wilson, "a team that's prepared to go the extra distance to do a good job."

"That's us!" said Tom.

"Well don't forget to lock up when you leave," said Mr Wilson as he turned to go.

"We won't," said Tom.

When the door closed, Sima burst out laughing. "Well, I suppose we haven't really told a lie," she said. "We are testing a game, aren't we?"

"Yes," said Kojo, "but not quite in the way Mr Wilson thinks!"

At one minute to midnight, Kojo handed out the headsets and the night-vision glasses.

"Put these on," he said, "and remember, we must all touch the screen at the same time to enter the game. It's only finished when we hear the words 'Game Over'. Just don't forget that you will only hear these words through your headsets."

"OK," said Tom and Sima.

Kojo loaded the game onto the computer. He checked his watch. It was just on the stroke of midnight. "Ready?" he asked.

"Ready!" said Tom and Sima.

They all put their hands on the screen and shut their eyes tightly as a bright light flashed. Then the light faded and they opened their eyes.

# CHAPTER 3

Kojo looked around. He couldn't see Tom or Sima anywhere.

"I must have made a mistake with the programming," said Kojo. "We've all been split up. I thought it was going too well. Keep in contact and let's try and work out where we are and how we can get back together. I'm in a big room with loads of old books. It must be the library. I can see something white moving about … this is really scary. Where are you two?"

"I think I'm in the basement. The walls have green slimy water seeping out of them. I can hear rats too. It's horrible!" said Tom.

"You're quite close to each other," said Sima. "The library is above the basement. Look for a large red book on a table, Kojo. Turn the book clockwise and a trapdoor will open by the table. Then you can drop down into the basement to get to Tom."

Kojo turned the book and the trapdoor opened. He dropped down into the basement just as Sima had thought.

"Nice one, Sima," said Tom. "Kojo's safe and sound."

"Right," said Sima. "Now look for a small passage at the far end of the basement. It ends in a staircase that should lead you out to the hallway. You'll see the main door there."

"But where are you, Sima? We can't leave you behind," cried Tom.

"I'm in a long corridor. It's really creepy," said Sima.

"Perhaps it leads to the main door, too," said Kojo.

"Go along the corridor. Don't stop whatever you do. Tom and I are on our way."

Tom and Kojo ran into the small passage at the back of the basement but it didn't lead to a staircase at all. Instead, it led into a room with a large fireplace at one end. The room was really dirty with cobwebs hanging from the ceiling and covering the furniture.

"This makes your flat look clean, Kojo" laughed Tom.

"Ha, ha!" sighed Kojo. "Very funny!"

Just then, they heard voices and music. Tom went over to the fireplace.

"It's coming from behind here," he said. "Listen. It sounds as if someone's having a party."

Kojo joined him at the fireplace. They pressed their heads against it to hear better, but as they did so, there was a loud click and it spun round. The boys stared open-mouthed. They were standing in a large ballroom, with a huge chandelier hanging from the ceiling. People were dancing to a band of musicians. The women wore old-fashioned gowns and the men wore breeches with velvet jackets — and they all had huge wigs on their heads!

39:00

click!

"It must be a fancy dress party," said Tom, tapping his foot in time to the music. "It looks cool."

"It's not cool at all," said Kojo. "This is much more sinister. Look!"

He pointed to the dancers' feet. None of them were touching the floor. Tom and Kojo watched in horror as the dancers floated above the ground. Worse still, as they passed under the chandelier, Tom and Kojo could see right through their bodies.

"You … you know what they are, d—d—don't you?" stuttered Kojo. "Th—they're …"

"Ghosts!" yelled Tom. "Run for it!"

# CHAPTER 4

Meanwhile, Sima was edging slowly along the corridor. It got narrower and narrower. The walls were lined with old portraits and the faces stared down at her. As she went past the pictures, the mouths moved and the eyes followed her.

Sima gulped. "I can't do this, guys," she said. No one answered.

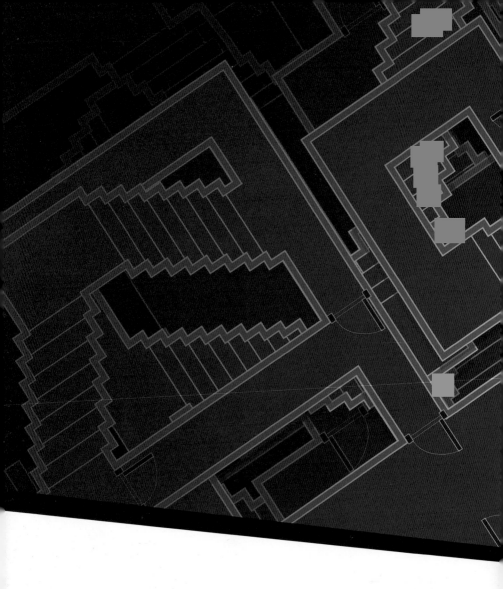

Tom and Kojo ran through a door at the back of the ballroom and into a small passage. It was hot and dark inside and their footsteps echoed around them. They ran on and on, but every time they turned a corner a new wall appeared in front of them.

Sima tapped at her headset. Nothing! It had stopped working. She began to panic and ran down the corridor. It got colder and colder, then something wet and slimy brushed across her face. She heard voices nearby whisper her name.

Sima ran faster and faster. She saw a staircase in front of her and ran towards it. She heard footsteps chasing after her and a loud groaning, moaning noise.

Suddenly, she felt ice-cold breath on her neck and hands grabbed at her. Then she heard the words 'Game Over, Game Over' being shrieked into her ear. Pulling off her headset, Sima ran down the stairs, but they were booby-trapped. A huge hole opened up and Sima screamed as she tumbled down into the darkness. She hit her head on the stone floor and blacked out.

A few minutes later, Sima came round. She could make out the main door in front of her. She tried to crawl towards it, but every time she got closer, the door moved further away.

Sima felt sick with fear. "I've lost my headset and the game must be over by now. I'm stuck in this house forever," she thought.

7:00

The air around her became colder and colder, and she began to feel sleepy.

I MUST KEEP AWAKE. IF I FALL ASLEEP NOW I'LL NEVER WAKE UP AGAIN.

Tom and Kojo heard Sima's screams as she fell.

SIMA MUST BE ON THE OTHER SIDE OF THIS WALL. HOW CAN WE REACH HER?

Kojo looked at his watch. "Oh no," he said. "There's less than five minutes of game time left. What are we going to do?"

"We've got to help her," yelled Tom. "I won't let anything happen to Sima." He punched the wall angrily with his fist, and as he did so a small section of the wooden panelling creaked open.

The boys peered through the gap and saw Sima lying on the floor. She was pale and barely breathing. Banging as hard as they could with their fists, the boys broke through the panelling.

Tom ran over to Sima. "Kojo, help me carry her through the main door," he yelled.

Kojo looked at his watch. "We'll never do it," he said. "We've only got three seconds left!"

Quickly, Tom grabbed Sima and ran through the door just as a bright light flashed and the words 'Game Over' played loudly in their headsets.

1:00

41

# CHAPTER 5

Back in the office, Tom bathed Sima's forehead with cold water.

"I don't understand it," she said. "I heard 'Game Over' in my headset over and over again. Then I fell through the stairs and the headset was gone. I thought I was going to be stuck in the house forever."

Kojo shrugged his shoulders. "I don't understand it either," he said. "We heard the 'Game Over' message just before we arrived back here. It couldn't have played before then." He picked up Sima's headset and examined it carefully. "This isn't damaged at all."

Sima and Tom looked at each other. Sima shivered.

"If I didn't hear the message from the headset, it must have been ..." she started.

"Yes," whispered Tom. "It must have been a ghost."

Kojo looked at his watch. "It's nearly two o'clock in the morning," he said. "It's time we went home for some sleep."

"I'm not going home alone now," said Sima. "I'm much too scared."

"Let's all sleep here tonight," suggested Tom.

"Good plan," said Sima, "but I'm not sleeping in the dark. Tonight, we're going to leave all the lights ON!"

# Glossary of terms

**basement**  part of a building that is below the ground level

**blacked out**  to become unconscious

**booby-trapped**  something hidden to catch someone unawares and hurt them

**breeches**  short trousers that are worn fastened below the knee

**chandelier**  a large hanging light with several branches

**cower(ing)**  to curl yourself up in a ball because you are frightened of someone or something

**gadget(s)**  a small tool or piece of equipment that is useful

**headset(s)**  headphones which may have a microphone attached

**night-vision glasses**  special glasses that help you to see in the dark

**overtime**  extra hours that a person works in their job

**panelling**  panels of wood used to cover walls

**portrait(s)**  a painting or drawing of a person

**practical**  if something is practical it is useful

**section**  an area within a larger place

**seeping**  flowing in or out of something, usually through small holes

**tweaks**  small adjustments

# Quiz

1 What was the name of the haunted house in the DVD?

2 Where did Tom and Kojo hide when the film got scary?

3 How many players was the new game designed for?

4 Where was the game set?

5 What gadgets were needed to play the game?

6 In which room did Kojo find himself at the start of the game?

7 Where did Tom and Kojo end up after they escaped the ballroom?

8 How were the stairs booby-trapped?

9 What made the section of panelling open up?

10 Where did Tom, Sima and Kojo sleep after the game?

# ABOUT THE AUTHOR

**Sue Graves** has taught for thirty years in Cheshire schools. She has been writing for more than ten years and has written well over a hundred books for children and young adults.

"Nearly everyone loves computer games. They are popular with all age groups – especially young adults. But I've often thought it would be amazing to play a computer game for real. To be in on the action would be the best experience ever! That's why I wrote these stories. I hope you enjoy reading them as much as I've enjoyed writing them for you."

# ANSWERS TO QUIZ

1  Chillington Mansion

2  Behind the sofa

3  Three

4  A haunted house called Midnight Mansion

5  Night-vision glasses and headsets

6  The library

7  A maze of corridors

8  They opened up into a big hole

9  Tom hit it with his fist

10  The office